Ruby the Red Fairy

Dedicated to Joanna Pilkington,
who found fairies in her
beautiful garden

Special thanks to
Narinder Dhami

No part of this publication may be reproduced, stored in
a retrieval system, or transmitted in any form or by any means,
electronic, mechanical, photocopying, recording, or otherwise, without
written permission of the publisher. For information regarding
permission, write to Working Partners Limited, 1 Albion Place,
London, W6OQT, United Kingdom.

ISBN 0-439-73861-X

Copyright © 2003 by Working Partners Limited.

Illustrations copyright © 2003 by Georgie Ripper.

All rights reserved. Published by Scholastic Inc., 557 Broadway,
New York, NY 10012, by arrangement with Working Partners
Limited.

SCHOLASTIC, LITTLE APPLE, and associated logos are
trademarks and/or registered trademarks of Scholastic Inc.

12 11 10 9 8 7 6 5 4 3   5 6 7 8 9 10/0

Printed in the U.S.A.

Ruby the Red Fairy

by Daisy Meadows

illustrated by Georgie Ripper

SCHOLASTIC INC.

New York   Toronto   London   Auckland   Sydney
Mexico City   New Delhi   Hong Kong   Buenos Aires

Cold winds blow and thick ice forms,
I conjure up this fairy storm.
To seven corners of the mortal world
the Rainbow Fairies will be hurled!

I curse every part of Fairyland,
with a frosty wave of my icy hand.
For now and always, from this fateful day,
Fairyland will be cold and gray!

Contents

The End of the Rainbow

"Look, Dad!" said Rachel Walker. She pointed across the blue-green sea at the rocky island ahead of them. The ferry was sailing toward it, dipping up and down on the rolling waves. "Is that Rainspell Island?" she asked.

Her dad nodded. "Yes, it is," he said, smiling. "Our vacation is about to begin!"

The waves slapped against the side
of the ferry as it bobbed up and down
on the water. Rachel felt her heart
thump with excitement. She could see
white cliffs and emerald-green fields on
the island. And golden sandy beaches,
with rock pools dotted here and there.

Suddenly, a few fat raindrops
plopped down onto Rachel's head.
"Oh!" she gasped, surprised. The sun
was still shining.

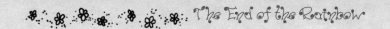

Rachel's mom grabbed her hand. "Let's get under cover," she said, leading Rachel inside.

"Isn't that strange?" Rachel said. "Sunshine *and* rain!"

"Let's hope the rain stops before we get off the ferry," said Mr. Walker. "Now, where did I put that map of the island?"

Rachel looked out of the window. Her eyes opened wide.

A girl was standing alone on the deck. Her dark hair was wet with raindrops, but she didn't seem to care. She just stared up at the sky.

Rachel looked over at her mom and
dad. They were busy studying the map.
So Rachel slipped back outside to see
what was so interesting.

And there it was.

In the blue sky, high above them,
was the most amazing rainbow that
Rachel had ever seen. One end of the
rainbow was far out to sea. The other
seemed to fall somewhere on Rainspell
Island. All of the colors were bright
and clear.

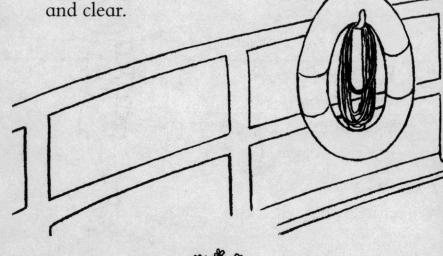

Red
Orange
Yellow
Green
Blue
Indigo
Violet

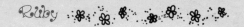

"Isn't it perfect?" the dark-haired girl whispered to Rachel.

"Yes, it is," Rachel agreed. "Are you going to Rainspell on vacation?"

The girl nodded. "We're staying for a week," she said. "I'm Kirsty Tate."

Rachel smiled as the rain began to stop. "I'm Rachel Walker. We're staying at Mermaid Cottage," she added.

"And we're at Dolphin Cottage," said Kirsty. "Do you think we might be near each other?"

"I hope so," Rachel replied. She had a feeling she was going to like Kirsty.

Kirsty leaned over the rail and looked down into the shimmering water. "The sea looks really deep, doesn't it?" she said. "There might even be mermaids down there, watching us right now!"

Rachel stared at the waves. She saw something that made her heart skip a beat. "Look!" she said. "Is that a mermaid's hair?" Then she laughed when she saw that it was just seaweed.

"It could be a mermaid's necklace," said Kirsty, smiling. "Maybe she lost it when she was trying to escape from a sea monster."

The ferry was now sailing
into Rainspell's tiny
harbor. Seagulls flew
around them, and fishing
boats bobbed
on the water.
"Look at
that big white cliff
over there," Kirsty
said. She pointed
it out to Rachel.
"It looks a bit
like a giant's
face, doesn't it?"
Rachel
looked, and
nodded. Kirsty
seemed to see magic
everywhere.

"There you are, Rachel!" called Mrs. Walker. Rachel turned around and saw her mom and dad coming out onto the deck. "We'll be getting off the ferry in a few minutes," Mrs. Walker added.

"Mom, Dad, this is Kirsty," Rachel said. "She's staying at Dolphin Cottage."

"That's right next door to ours," said Mr. Walker. "I remember seeing it on the map."

Rachel and Kirsty looked at each other in delight.

"I'd better go and find *my* mom and dad," said Kirsty. She looked around. "Oh, here they are."

Kirsty's mom and dad came over
to say hello to the Walkers. Then the
ferry docked, and everyone began to
leave the boat.

"Our cottages are on the other side
of the harbor," said Rachel's dad,
looking at the map. "It's not far."

Mermaid Cottage and Dolphin
Cottage were right next to the beach.
Rachel loved her bedroom, which was
high up, in the attic. From the
window, she could see the waves
rolling onto the sand.

A shout from outside made her look down. It was Kirsty. She was standing under the window, waving at her.

"Let's go and explore the beach!" Kirsty called.

Rachel dashed outside to join her.

Seaweed lay in piles on the sand, and there were tiny pink-and-white shells dotted about.

"I love it here already!" Rachel shouted happily above the noise of the seagulls.

"Me, too," Kirsty said. She pointed up at the sky. "Look, the rainbow's still there."

Rachel looked up. The rainbow glowed brightly among the fluffy white clouds.

"Have you heard the story about the pot of gold at the end of the rainbow?" Kirsty asked.

Rachel nodded. "Yes, but that's just in fairy tales," she said.

Kirsty grinned. "Maybe. But let's go and find out for ourselves!"

"OK," Rachel agreed. "We can explore the island at the same time."

They rushed back to tell their parents where they were going. Then Kirsty and Rachel set off along a road behind the cottages. It led them away from the beach, across green fields, and toward a small woods.

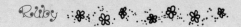

Rachel kept looking up at the rainbow. She was worried that it would start to fade now that the rain had stopped. But the colors stayed clear and bright.

"It looks like the end of the rainbow is over there," Kirsty said. "Come on!" And she hurried toward the trees.

The woods were cool and green after the heat of the sun. Rachel and Kirsty followed a winding path until they came to a clearing. Then they both stopped and stared.

The rainbow shone down onto the grass through a gap in the trees.

And there, at the rainbow's end, lay an old, black pot.

A Tiny Surprise

"Look!" Kirsty whispered. "There really is a pot of gold!"

"It could just be a cooking pot," Rachel said doubtfully. "Some campers might have left it behind."

But Kirsty shook her head. "I don't think so," she said. "It looks really old."

Rachel stared at the pot. It was sitting on the grass, upside down.

"Let's have a closer look," said Kirsty. She ran to the pot and tried to turn it over. "Oh, it's heavy!" she gasped. She tried again, but the pot didn't move.

Rachel rushed to help her. They both pushed and pushed at the pot. This time it moved, just a little.

"Let's try again." Kirsty panted. "Are you ready, Rachel?"

Tap! Tap! Tap!

Rachel and Kirsty stared at each other.

"What was that?" Rachel gasped.

"I don't know," whispered Kirsty.

Tap! Tap!

"There it is again," Kirsty said. She looked down at the pot lying on the grass. "You know what? I think it's coming from inside this pot!"

Rachel's eyes opened wide. "Are you sure?" She bent down, and put her ear to the pot. *Tap! Tap!* Then, to her amazement, Rachel heard a tiny voice.

"Help!" it called. "Help me!"

Rachel grabbed Kirsty's arm. "Did you hear that?" she asked.

Kirsty nodded. "Quick!" she said. "We have to turn the pot over!"

Rachel and Kirsty pushed at the pot as hard as they could. It began to rock from side to side on the grass.

"We're almost there!" Rachel panted.
"Keep pushing, Kirsty!"

The girls pushed with all their might.
Suddenly, the pot turned over and
rolled onto its side. Rachel and Kirsty
were taken by surprise. They both lost
their balance and landed on the grass
with a thump.

"Look!" Kirsty whispered, breathing
hard.

A small shower of sparkling red dust
had flown out of the pot.
Rachel and Kirsty gasped
with surprise. The dust
hung in the air above
them. And there, right in
the middle of the glittering
cloud, was a tiny, winged girl.

Rachel and Kirsty watched in wonder as the tiny girl fluttered in the sunlight, her delicate wings sparkling with all the colors of the rainbow.

"Oh, Rachel!" Kirsty whispered. "It's a fairy. . . ."

Fairy Magic

The fairy flew over Rachel's and Kirsty's heads. Her short, silky dress was the color of ripe strawberries. Red crystal earrings glowed in her ears. Her golden hair was braided with tiny red roses, and her little feet wore crimson slippers.

She waved her scarlet wand, and the shower of sparkling red fairy dust floated

softly down to the ground. Where
it landed, all sorts of red flowers
appeared with a *pop!*

Rachel and Kirsty watched
openmouthed. It really and truly *was*
a fairy.

"This is like a dream," Rachel said.

"I always believed in fairies," Kirsty
whispered back. "But I never thought
I'd ever *see* one!"

The fairy flew toward them. "Oh,
thank you *so* much!" she called in a
tiny, silvery voice. "I'm free at last!"
She glided down, and landed on
Kirsty's hand.

Kirsty gasped. The fairy felt lighter
and softer than a butterfly.

"I was beginning to think I'd *never*
get out of that pot!" the fairy said.

Kirsty wanted to ask the fairy so
many things. But she didn't know
where to start.

"Tell me your names, quickly," said
the fairy. She fluttered up into the air
again. "There's so much to be done,
and we must get started right away."

Rachel wondered what the fairy
meant. "I'm Rachel," she said.

"And I'm Kirsty," said Kirsty. "But
who are *you*?"

"I'm the Red Rainbow Fairy — but call
me Ruby," the fairy replied.

"Ruby . . ." Kirsty breathed. "A
Rainbow Fairy . . ." She and Rachel
stared at each other in excitement.
This really *was* magic!

"Yes," said Ruby. "And I have six
sisters: Amber, Saffron, Fern, Sky, Inky,
and Heather. One for each color of
the rainbow, you see."

"What do Rainbow Fairies do?"
Rachel asked.

Ruby flew over and landed lightly on
Rachel's hand. "It's our job to put all the
different colors into Fairyland," she
explained.

"So why were you shut up inside
that old pot?" asked Rachel.

"And where are your sisters?" Kirsty
added.

Ruby's golden wings drooped. Her
eyes filled with tiny, sparkling tears.
"I don't know," she said. "Something
terrible has happened in Fairyland. We
really need your help!"

Fairies in Danger

Kirsty stared down at Ruby, sitting sadly
on Rachel's hand. "Of course we'll help
you!" she said.

"Just tell us how," added Rachel.

Ruby wiped the tears from her eyes.
"Thank you!" she said. "But first I must
show you the terrible thing that has
happened. Follow me — as quickly as

you can!" She flew into the air, her
wings shimmering in the
sunshine.

Rachel and Kirsty
followed Ruby across the
clearing. She danced
ahead of them,
glowing like a
crimson flame. She
stopped at a small
pond under a
weeping willow tree.
"Look! I can show
you what happened
yesterday," she said.

She flew over the
pond and scattered another
shower of sparkling fairy dust
with her tiny, red wand. All at once,

the water lit up with a strange,
silver light. It bubbled and
fizzed, and then became still.
With wide eyes, Rachel
and Kirsty watched as
a picture appeared.
It was like looking
through a window into
another land!
"Oh, Rachel,
look!" said Kirsty.
A river of the
brightest blue ran
swiftly past hills of the
greenest green. Scattered
on the hillsides were red-
and-white toadstool houses.
And on top of the highest hill stood a
silver palace with four pink towers.

The towers were so high, their points were almost hidden by the fluffy white clouds floating past.

Hundreds of fairies were making their way toward the palace. Some were walking and some were flying. Rachel and Kirsty could see goblins, elves, imps, and pixies, too. Everyone seemed very excited.

"Yesterday was the day of the Fairyland Midsummer Ball," Ruby explained. She flew over the pond and pointed down with her wand to a spot in the middle of the scene. "There I am, with my Rainbow sisters."

Kirsty and Rachel looked closely at where Ruby was pointing. They saw seven fairies, each dressed prettily in her own rainbow color. Wherever

they flew, they left a trail of fairy dust
behind them.

"The Midsummer Ball is *very*
special," Ruby went on. "And my
sisters and I are always in charge of
sending out invitations."

To the sound of tinkling music, the
front doors of the palace slowly opened.

"Here come King Oberon and Queen
Titania," said Ruby. "The Fairy King
and Queen. They are about to begin
the ball."

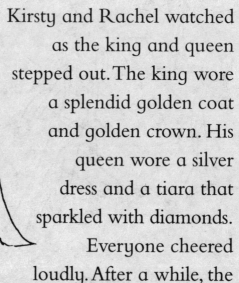

Kirsty and Rachel watched
as the king and queen
stepped out. The king wore
a splendid golden coat
and golden crown. His
queen wore a silver
dress and a tiara that
sparkled with diamonds.
Everyone cheered
loudly. After a while, the
king signaled for quiet. "Fairies," he
began. "We are very glad to see you all
here. Welcome to the Midsummer Ball!"

The fairies clapped their hands and
cheered again. A band of green frogs in
smart purple outfits started to play, and
the dancing began.

Suddenly, a gray mist seemed to fill the
room. Kirsty and Rachel watched in
alarm as all the fairies started to shiver.
And a loud, chilly voice shouted out,
"Stop the music!"

The band fell silent. Everyone looked
scared. A tall, bony figure was pushing
his way through the crowd. He was
dressed all in white, and there was frost
on his white hair and beard. But his face
was red and angry.

"Who's that?" Rachel asked with a shiver. Ice had begun to form around the edge of the pond.

"It's Jack Frost," said Ruby. And she shivered, too.

Jack Frost glared at the seven Rainbow Fairies. "Why wasn't I invited to the Midsummer Ball?" he asked coldly.

The Rainbow Fairies gasped in horror. . . .

Ruby looked up from the pond picture. She smiled sadly at Rachel and Kirsty. "Yes, we forgot to invite Jack Frost," she said.

The Fairy Queen stepped forward. "You are very welcome, Jack Frost," she said. "Please stay and enjoy the ball."

But Jack Frost looked even more
angry. "Too late!" he hissed. "You
forgot to invite me!" He turned and
pointed a thin, icy finger at the
Rainbow Fairies.

"Well, you will not forget this!" he went on. "My spell will banish the Rainbow Fairies to the seven corners of the mortal world. From this day on, Fairyland will be without color — forever!"

Jack Frost's Spell

As Jack Frost cast his spell, a great, icy wind began to blow. It picked up the seven Rainbow Fairies and spun them up into the darkening sky. The other fairies watched in dismay.

Jack Frost turned to the king and queen. "Your Rainbow Fairies will be trapped, never to return." With that, he left, leaving a trail of icy footprints.

Quickly, the Fairy Queen stepped forward and lifted her silver wand. "I cannot undo Jack Frost's magic completely," she shouted, as the wind howled and rushed around her. "But I can guide the Rainbow Fairies to a safe place until they can be rescued!"

The queen pointed her wand at the

gray sky overhead. A black pot came spinning through the stormy clouds. It flew toward the Rainbow Fairies. One by one, the Rainbow Fairies tumbled into the pot.

"Pot-at-the-end-of-the-rainbow, keep our Rainbow Fairies safely together," the queen called. "And take them to Rainspell Island!"

The pot flew out of sight, behind a dark cloud. And the bright colors of Fairyland began to fade, until it looked like an old black-and-white photograph.

"Oh, no!" Kirsty gasped. Then the picture in the pond vanished.

"So the Fairy Queen cast her *own* spell!" Rachel said. She was bursting with questions. "She put you and your sisters in the pot, and sent you to Rainspell."

Ruby nodded. "Our queen knew that we would be safe here," she said. "We know Rainspell well. It is a place full of magic."

"But where are your sisters?" Kirsty wanted to know. "They were in the pot, too."

Ruby looked upset. "Jack Frost's spell
must have been stronger than the
queen thought," she said. "As the pot
spun through the sky, the wind blew
my sisters out again. I was at the
bottom, so I was safe. But I was
trapped when the pot landed upside
down."

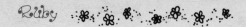

"So are your sisters somewhere on Rainspell?" Kirsty asked.

Ruby nodded. "Yes, but they're scattered all over the island. Jack Frost's spell has trapped them, too." She flew toward Kirsty and landed on her shoulder. "That's where you and Rachel come in."

"How?" Rachel asked.

"You found *me,* didn't you?" the fairy went on. "That's because you believe in magic." She flew from Kirsty's shoulder to Rachel's. "So, you could rescue my Rainbow sisters, too! Then we can all bring color back to Fairyland again."

A Visit to Fairyland

"Of course we'll search for your sisters," Kirsty said quickly. "Won't we, Rachel?"

Rachel nodded.

"Oh, thank you," Ruby said happily.

"But we're only here for a week," Rachel said. "Will that be long enough?"

"We have to get started right away,"

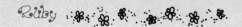

said Ruby. "First, I must take you to
Fairyland to meet our king and
queen. They will be very pleased to
know that you are going to help me
find my sisters."

Rachel and Kirsty stared at Ruby.

"You're taking us to *Fairyland*?"
Kirsty gasped. She could hardly believe
her ears. Nor could Rachel.

"But how will we get there?" Rachel
wanted to know.

"We'll fly there," Ruby replied.

"But *we* can't fly!" Rachel pointed
out.

Ruby smiled. She whirled up into
the air and flew over the girls'
heads. Then she swirled her wand
above them. Magic red fairy dust
fluttered down.

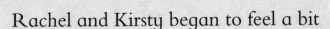

Rachel and Kirsty began to feel a bit
strange. Were the trees
getting bigger or were
they getting smaller?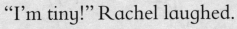

They were getting smaller!
Smaller and smaller and
smaller, until they were
the same size as Ruby.

"I'm tiny!" Rachel laughed.
She was so small, the flowers around
her seemed like trees.

Kirsty twisted around to look at her
back. She had wings —
shiny and delicate
as a butterfly's!
Ruby beamed
at them. "Now
you can fly," she
said. "Let's go."

Rachel twitched her shoulders. Her
wings fluttered, and she felt herself rise up
into the air. She felt quite wobbly at first.
It was very odd!

"Help!" Kirsty yelled, as she shot up
into the air. "I'm not very good at this!"

"Come on," said Ruby, taking their
hands. "I'll help you." She led them up,
out of the glade.

Rachel looked down on Rainspell
Island. She could see the cottages next to
the beach, and the harbor.

"Where *is* Fairyland, Ruby?" Kirsty asked. They were flying higher and higher, up into the clouds.

"It's so far away that no mortal could ever find it," Ruby said.

They flew on through the clouds for a long, long time. But at last Ruby turned to them and smiled. "We're here," she said.

As they flew down from the clouds, Kirsty and Rachel saw places they recognized from the pond picture: the palace, the hillsides with their toadstool houses, the river and flowers. But there were no bright colors now. Because of Jack Frost's spell, everything was a drab shade of gray. Even the air felt cold and damp.

A few fairies walked miserably across
the hillsides. Their wings hung limply
down their backs. No one could
be bothered to fly.

Suddenly, one of the fairies looked up
into the sky. "Look!" she shouted. "It's
Ruby. She's come back!"

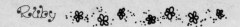

At once, the fairies flew up toward
Ruby, Kirsty, and Rachel. They circled
around them, looking much happier,
and asking lots of questions.

"Have you come from Rainspell,
Ruby?"

"Where are the other Rainbow
Fairies?"

"Who are your friends?"

"First, we must see the king and
queen. Then I will tell you
everything!" Ruby promised.

King Oberon and Queen Titania were seated on their thrones. Their palace was as gray and gloomy as everything else in Fairyland. But they smiled warmly when Ruby arrived with Rachel and Kirsty.

"Welcome back, Ruby," the queen said. "We have missed you."

"Your Majesties, I have found two mortals who believe in magic!" Ruby announced. "These are my friends Kirsty and Rachel."

Quickly, Ruby explained what had happened to the other Rainbow Fairies. She told everyone how Rachel and Kirsty had rescued her.

"You have our thanks," the king told them. "Our Rainbow Fairies are very special to us."

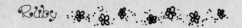

"And will you help us to find Ruby's
Rainbow sisters?" the queen asked.

"Yes, we will," Kirsty said.

"But how will we know where to
look?" Rachel wanted to know.

"The trick is not to look too hard,"
said Queen Titania. "Don't worry.
As you enjoy the rest of your vacation,
the magic you need to find each
Rainbow Fairy will find *you*. Just
wait and see."

King Oberon rubbed his beard
thoughtfully. "You have six days of
your vacation left, and six fairies to
find," he said. "A fairy each day.
That's a lot of fairy-finding. You
will need some special help." He
nodded at one of his footmen, a
plump frog in a buttoned-up jacket.

The frog hopped over to Rachel and
Kirsty and handed them each a tiny,
silver bag.

"The bags contain magic tools," the
queen told them. "Don't look inside
them yet. Open them only when you
really need to, and you will find
something to help you." She smiled at
Kirsty and Rachel.

"Look!" shouted another frog
footman suddenly. "Ruby is beginning
to fade!"

Rachel and Kirsty looked at Ruby in
horror. The fairy was growing paler
before their eyes. Her lovely dress was
no longer red, but pink, and her golden
hair was turning white.

"Jack Frost's magic is still at work," said the king, looking worried. "We cannot undo his spell until the Rainbow Fairies are all together again."

"Quickly, Ruby!" urged the queen. "You must return to Rainspell at once."

Ruby, Kirsty, and Rachel rose into the air, their wings fluttering.

"Don't worry!" Kirsty called, as they flew higher. "We'll be back with all the Rainbow Fairies very soon!"

"Good luck!" called the king and queen.

Rachel and Kirsty watched Ruby worriedly as they flew off. But as they got farther away from Fairyland, Ruby's color began to return. Soon she was bright and sparkling again.

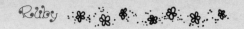

They reached Rainspell at last. Ruby
led Rachel and Kirsty to the clearing
in the woods, and they landed
next to the old, black pot.
Then Ruby scattered
fairy dust over
Rachel and Kirsty.
There was a puff of
glittering red smoke,
and the two girls
shot up to their
normal size again.
Rachel wriggled
her shoulders. Yes,
her wings were gone.
"Oh, I really *loved*
being a fairy," Kirsty said.
They watched as Ruby sprinkled her
magic dust over the old, black pot.

"What are you doing?" Rachel asked.

"Jack Frost's magic means that I can't help you look for my sisters," Ruby replied sadly. "So I will wait for you here, in the pot-at-the-end-of-the-rainbow."

Suddenly, the pot began to move. It rolled across the grass and stopped under the weeping willow tree. The tree's branches hung right down to the ground.

"The pot will be hidden under the tree," Ruby explained. "I'll be safe there."

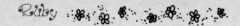

"We'd better start looking for the other Rainbow Fairies," Rachel said to Kirsty. "Where shall we start?"

Ruby shook her head. "Remember what the queen said," she told them. "The magic will come to you." She flew over and sat on the edge of the pot. Then she pushed aside one of the willow branches and waved at Rachel and Kirsty. "Good-bye, and good luck!"

"We'll be back soon, Ruby," Kirsty promised.

"We're going to find all of your Rainbow sisters," Rachel said firmly. "Just you wait and see!"

Ruby is safely hidden in the
pot-at-the-end-of-the-rainbow.
Now Rachel and Kirsty must find

Amber the Orange Fairy

A Very Unusual Shell

"What a lovely day!" Rachel Walker shouted, staring up at the blue sky. She and her friend Kirsty Tate were running along Rainspell Island's yellow, sandy beach. Their parents walked a little way behind them.

"It's a *magical* day," Kirsty added. The two friends smiled at each other.

Rachel and Kirsty had come to
Rainspell Island for their vacations.
They had soon found out it really
was a magical place!

As they ran, they passed rock pools
that shone like jewels in the sunshine.

Rachel spotted a little *splash!* in one of
the pools. "There's something in there,
Kirsty!" She pointed. "Let's go and
look."

The girls jogged over to the pool and
crouched down to see.

Kirsty's heart thumped as she gazed
into the crystal-clear water. "What is
it?" she asked.

Suddenly, the water rippled. A little
brown crab scuttled sideways across
the sandy bottom and vanished under
a rock.

Kirsty felt disappointed. "I thought it might be another Rainbow Fairy," she said.

"So did I." Rachel sighed. "Never mind. We'll keep on looking."

"Of course we will," Kirsty agreed. Then she put her finger to her lips as their parents came up behind them. *"Shhh."*

Kirsty and Rachel had a big secret. They were helping to find the Rainbow Fairies. Thanks to Jack Frost's wicked spell, the fairies were lost on Rainspell Island. And until they were all found, there would be no color in Fairyland.

Rachel looked at the shimmering blue sea. "Do you want to go swimming?" she asked.

But Kirsty wasn't listening. She was shading her eyes with her hand and looking farther along the beach. "Over there, Rachel — by those rocks," she said.

Then Rachel could see it, too — something winking and sparkling in the sunshine. "Wait for me!" she called, as Kirsty hurried over there.

When they saw what it was, the two friends sighed in disappointment.

"It's just the wrapper from a chocolate bar," Rachel said sadly. She bent down and picked up the shiny purple foil.

Kirsty thought for a moment. "Do you remember what the Fairy Queen said?" she asked.

Rachel nodded. *"Let the magic come to you,"* she said. "You're right, Kirsty. We should just enjoy our vacation, and wait for the magic to happen."

Read the rest of

Amber the **Orange Fairy**

to find out what magic happens next. . . .